Whistling the Morning In

NEW POEMS BY LILLIAN MORRISON
ILLUSTRATIONS BY JOEL COOK

THE DAY OPENS

The day opens out.
The night closes in.
Sleep covers you.
Morning discovers you.

WORDSONG

BOOKS BY LILLIAN MORRISON

Poetry
The Ghosts of Jersey City
Miranda's Music (with Jean Boudin)
The Sidewalk Racer
Who Would Marry a Mineral?
Overheard in a Bubble Chamber
The Break Dance Kids

Folk Rhyme Collections
Yours Till Niagara Falls
Black Within and Red Without
A Diller, A Dollar
Touch Blue ·
Remember Me When This You See
Best Wishes, Amen

Poetry Anthologies
Sprints and Distances
Rhythm Road

Text copyright © 1992 by Lillian Morrison
Illustrations copyright © 1992 by Joel Cook
All rights reserved
Published by Wordsong
Boyds Mills Press, Inc., A Highlights Company
910 Church Street, Honesdale, Pennsylvania 18431
Publisher Cataloging-in-Publication Data
Morrison, Lillian.
Whistling the morning in/new poems by Lillian Morrison;
illustrations by Joel Cook.
(40)p. : col. ill. ;   cm.
Summary: An illustrated collection of nature poems, including
sights and sounds of the outdoors.
ISBN 1-56397-035-X.
1. Children's poetry, American. (1. American poetry.)
I. Cook, Joel, ill. II. Title.
811/.54 — dc20   1992
Library of Congress Catalog Card Number: 91-91409

First edition, 1992
Book designed by Joel Cook
Distributed by St. Martin's Press
Printed in Hong Kong
1   3   5   7   9   10   8   6   4   2

CONTENTS

For Jamie, Jennifer, Katie, Amy and Joey
L.M.

For Lucy, and all that that implies
J.C.

ACKNOWLEDGMENTS

Some of these poems have originally appeared in the following magazines—
BITS 3: "Outdoors" under the title "The Sun" ; COTTON BOLL/ATLANTA REVIEW:
"The Wildflowers"; HORN BOOK: "Autumn Morning," "Proposal," and "Literally";
SUNRUST: "Country Clothesline"; WATERWAYS: "Oh, to Be an Earthworm" and
"The Sun."
"Rain and Snow" first appeared in *To Ride a Butterfly*, an anthology published
by Bantam Doubleday Dell in 1991 for the benefit of Reading Is Fundamental.

whistling the morning in

ALL YOURS

When you hear birds
in the distance
whistling the morning in
you know that the sun
is about to decide
to let the day begin.

Last evening the sun
was drowning in dream,
now it's awake and new.
Seemingly shy, soon it
lights the whole sky
with a day to jump
                              in
                          to.

PROPOSAL

Let's give the breeze
honors for innovation,
for shaking things up
in the neighborhood,
for introducing new
interesting air
into our nostrils,
for travel too,
for going everywhere
without fear,
and for diplomacy,
making its presence known
so pleasantly
that it is almost always
well received.

THE SUN

Each evening
the sun
goes on a journey
under the world.

Each morning
he returns
a little weary
having been through
danger and dark places.

We greet him with
cheers and gratitude.
He grows and glows
for us, tall, taller.

A KIND OF TENDERNESS

A light rain
touches the window pane
with thinnest fingers.
A tear trickles
down the face of glass
where a fingertip lingers.

RAIN SOUND

At first it's like drumming
as it patters down, then stops.
Now it's an animal
outside the window
quietly licking its chops.

NOON

The summer sun
   is at its summit
moving toward
   its nightly plummet.

OUTDOORS

The sun is my mother.
She says, Hi Lily!
She knows me.
Are you really Lily, she says,
I thought you'd never come.

TWO PICTURES

THE ISLAND

Wrinkled stone
like an elephant's skin
on which young birches are treading.

THE BIRDS

Two snow geese flying
in the crystal space
between forest and storm cloud.

DAILY VIOLENCE

Dawn cracked;
  the sun stole through.
Day broke;
  the sun climbed over rooftops.
Clouds chased the sun,
  then burst.
Night fell.
The clock struck midnight.

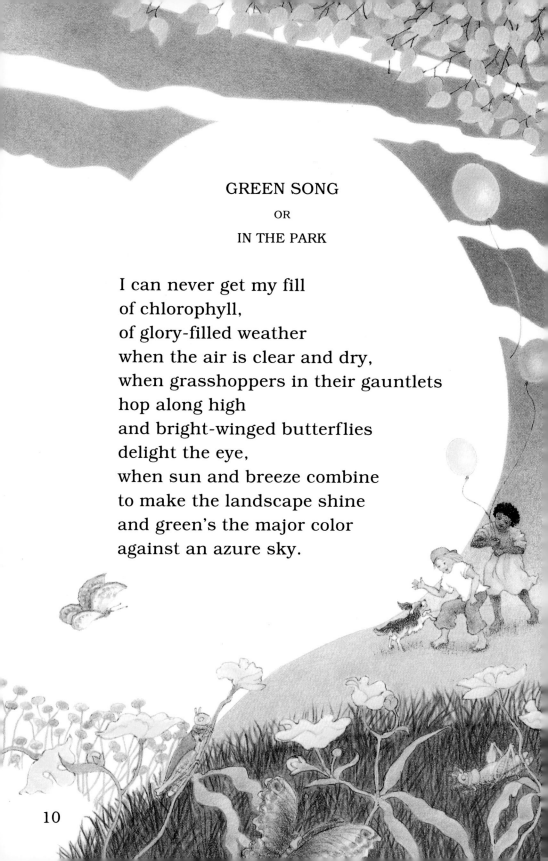

GREEN SONG

OR

IN THE PARK

I can never get my fill
of chlorophyll,
of glory-filled weather
when the air is clear and dry,
when grasshoppers in their gauntlets
hop along high
and bright-winged butterflies
delight the eye,
when sun and breeze combine
to make the landscape shine
and green's the major color
against an azure sky.

10

THE POPPLE TREE

I sing the elongated popple,
so thin it's like to topple.
I wonder if it's supple,
bendable like birches.
In any case it serves
for birds who like tall perches.

THE WILDFLOWERS

Orange-yellow
among the green,
the jewel-weed dangles

but summer is passing;
the spiky-spired fireweed
is going to seed

and thistle flowers,
cotton-covered,
no longer stand explicit.

Late summer
has a ragged edge,
here a bright tatter

there a bit of old lace
waving goodbye.

AUTUMN MORNING

Someone is pressing
the waking switches,
lights in the brain
go on, one by one,
two by two, ten by ten,
a floodlight, your eyes
are open, the sun
pours in, the tulip
tree outside the window
is one great glob
of YELLOW!

COUNTRY CLOTHESLINE

OR

AFTER THE QUARREL

Snap, bedsheets,
flap on the swaying line.
The wind that whips
and ripples you to drying
that teases towels
and bends the buttercups
is tripping us up too.

All that was stiff
has fallen on its face
lost in the waving grass.
Washed, blown,
we're pliable now,
bright-eyed and trim
like the daisies.

THE GREETING

Sometimes after a heavy rain
or after a morning of snow
the sun shoots out from behind a cloud
with a great big hot Hello!

SLEDDING

There's nothing like the thrill,
eyes popping, heart bop-bopping,
    of
        whizzing
          down
            a
          long
              snowy
                hill
                 belly-whopping!

MORNING ON THE BEACH

Foam bubbles
and a wet corsage,
mementos of a party
the sea threw last night.
You should have seen
the dolphins dance
and heard the thunder drum.
Mermaids sang and sang
to waves' crashing applause.
What carryings on!
The moon showed up late
in silver and pearl
and dazzled the place.
When she went home
it all broke up.

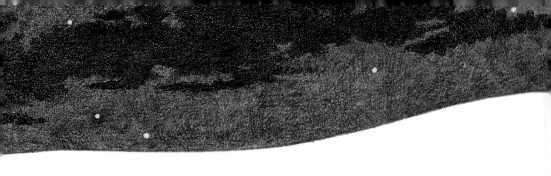

BREAKERS

Roaring,
all flowing grace,
the water tigers pounce,
feed on the shore,
worry it
again and again,
take great bites
they cannot swallow
and leave the toothmarks
of their long white fangs.

NEWS OF THE OCEAN

Today it is quiet,
wave heights good.
It's still rippling in
and pulling back
the way it should;
the planet's pulse
reminding us
it will go on
keeping its steady beat
when we're long gone.

RAIN AND SNOW

The rain comes down in stripes
And hits the ground in dots
And wets the streets and houses
And all the empty lots.

The snow comes down like feathers
Drifting through the sky
And lightly lays a blanket
On roads and passersby.

THE BOXING MATCH

Two bushes have come to blows.
The wind is egging them on.
Their shadows are boxing here on the rug
In a broad strip of sun.

Wham, wham, they bob and weave,
Then abruptly the battle is done.
The wind has rushed to another arena.
Nobody hurt. Nobody won.

THE MORNING MOON

The morning moon
allows the clouds
a game of hide and seek.

She hangs there, very
confident, very round
bland and sleek

watching the birds
flitting in and out
of the sycamore tree.

Why is she here?
Did she forget where she lives?
Did she lose her way?

Will she stay until
the sun comes back
from the other sky?

No, she's gone already
in the turn of your head
in the wink of your eye.

LITERALLY

If clouds were clods
and dreams were drams
the world would be
a dull word.

OH, TO BE AN EARTHWORM

Oh, to be an earthworm.
It has five hearts.
When one is pained or pierced
the other four carry on.
It has no chin to "take it" on
no upper lip, no backbone
to keep stiff, just crawls
along in closest touch with earth;
doesn't yearn at the stars
or stretch for the moon
but goes about its intimate
business, living its soft life
to the full, savoring it
inch by inch.

TUGBOAT AT DAYBREAK

The necklace of the bridge
is already dimmed for morning
but a tug in a tiara
glides slowly up the river,
a jewel of the dawn,
still festooned in light.

The river seems to slumber
quiet in its bed,
as silently the tugboat,
a ghostlike apparition,
moves twinkling up the river
and disappears from sight.

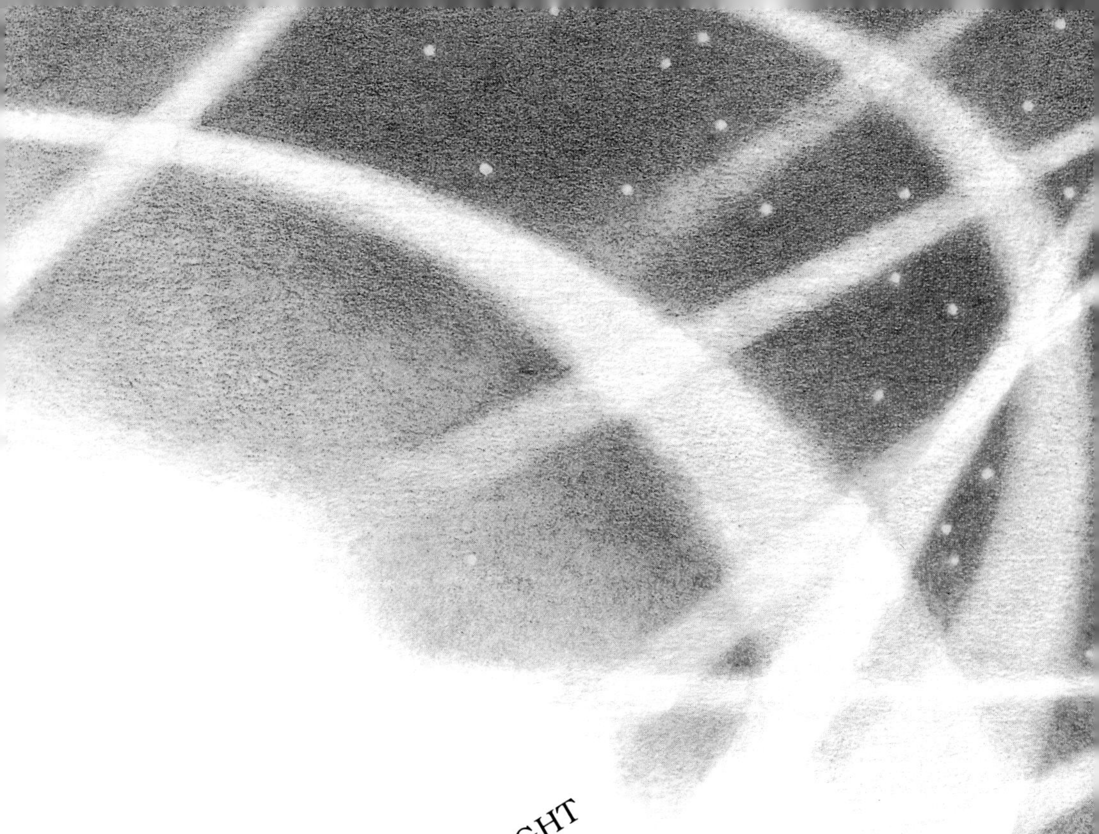

JET PLANES AT NIGHT

Their lights loom
in the dark sky
under the moon
as they zoom
serenading it with a roaring drone
in the distance
that dies away

GOING TO SLEEP

Sometimes I lie on my side,
hands clinging to a rope
looped round the hook
of wakefulness, until
an unseen finger lifts
the loop, casts off and
I float away, a light raft
on the breathing ocean.